The Ladybird Key Words Reading Scheme is based on these commonly used words. Those used most often in the English language are introduced first—with other words of popular appeal to children. All the Key Words list is covered in the early books, and the later titles use further word lists to develop full reading fluency. The total number of different words which will be learned in the complete reading scheme is nearly two thousand. The gradual introduction of these words, frequent repetition and complete 'carry-over' from book to book, will ensure rapid learning.

The full colour illustrations have been designed to create a desirable attitude towards learning— by making every child *eager* to read each title. Thus this attractive reading scheme embraces not only the latest findings in word frequency, but also the natural interests and activities of happy children.

Each book contains a list of the new words introduced.

W MURRAY, the author of the Ladybird Key Words Reading Scheme, is an experienced headmaster, author and lecturer on the teaching of reading. He is co-author, with J McNally, of Key Words to Literacy — a teacher's book published by The Teacher Publishing Co Ltd.

THE LADYBIRD KEY WORDS READING SCHEME has 12 graded books in each of its three series—'**a**', '**b**' and '**c**'. These 36 graded books are all written on a controlled vocabulary, and take the learner from the earliest stages of reading to reading fluency.

The '**a**' series gradually introduces and repeats new words. The parallel '**b**' series gives the needed further repetition of these words at each stage, but in a different context and with different illustrations.

The '**c**' series is also parallel to the '**a**' series, and supplies the necessary link with writing and phonic training.

An illustrated booklet—*Notes for using the Ladybird Key Words Reading Scheme*—can be obtained free from the publishers. This booklet fully explains the Key Words principle. It also includes information on the reading books, work books and apparatus available, and such details as the vocabulary loading and reading ages of all books.

BOOK 11a
The Ladybird Key Words Reading Scheme

Mystery
on the island

by W MURRAY

with illustrations
by MARTIN AITCHISON

Ladybird Books Loughborough

As Peter and Jane walked through the village they saw a policeman they knew. He came over to ask them if they had seen a boy he wanted to find.

"His name is Ron Dare," he said. "He's fourteen years old and he has red hair. You may know him as he used to stay near this village for his holidays."

Peter and Jane said that they did not know the boy and had not seen him. Peter asked the policeman why he wanted to find him.

"He's run away," he answered. "He hasn't been seen for a week. A little motor boat is missing from his father's holiday house near here, and I think the boy may have it."

After they had left the policeman, the brother and sister walked on towards the beach. They were going to help their cousins John and Simon to paint their motor boat. On the way they talked about the missing boy. "I'd like to help him," said Jane. "He can't be happy if he's run away like that. He won't be able to live on his own for very long if he's only fourteen."

"As he has red hair he should be found quite easily," said Peter.

John and Simon had just started work on their motor boat. It had been pulled away from the water's edge so that they could walk round it as they worked. Both the boys wore old clothes. They were glad to see their cousins arrive.

Peter and Jane also wore old clothes as they knew they would get dirty. It didn't worry them that they had to do some dirty work. They liked to help their cousins and work on the boat. They knew that they would soon go out to sea in it again.

Peter told his cousins about the policeman, the missing boy and the boat. Both John and Simon said that they hadn't seen the red haired boy or the boat. "I hope that he's not had an accident," said Simon.

After working for some time they stopped for a rest and to have the food and drink they had brought.

As they sat looking out to sea they saw some smoke a long way out. "What's that smoke?" asked Jane.

"It seems to come from the island," said Simon, "but nobody should be there. I think there's some-one on the island."

As soon as the paint on the motor boat and dinghy had dried, Peter, Jane and their two cousins went to the island. They wanted to see if anyone was there. They had no news of the missing boy and they thought he might be hiding on the island.

After they had pulled their dinghy up the beach, they looked around. At first they could see no sign that anyone had come to the island. Then they walked along the beach looking for signs of a boat, or footprints in the sand.

"Come over here!" Simon called to the others. "Come and look at this!" They all ran across to Simon, who was by some rocks.

"A footprint!" said John. "I don't think it's one of ours." Then each of them made a footprint by the one Simon had found. "Not one of them is the same," said John. "Ours are too small or too big."

"This footprint looks as if it might have been made by the boy who is missing," said Simon.

"First smoke and now the footprint," said John. "Let's look for a boat. If it's here it will mean that the boy is hiding on the island now."

Before they started to search for the boat, the four talked together.

"Could a boy pull a boat out of the water and hide it by himself?" asked John.

"Not a big boat," answered Simon. Then he asked, "How big is the missing boat?"

"The policeman said it was a very small dinghy with an outboard engine," said Peter.

"Then it could be done," said Simon. "Come on, everyone, let's start. Search the sands first for signs where the boat came out of the water."

Although they looked for some time they didn't find the boat. Simon called the others together and said, "I know what the boy has done. He's made the sand smooth again after the boat made marks on it."

"Yes," agreed John, "he may have smoothed out the marks, so that nobody would know he was here. Search further away from the water!"

After a few minutes the others heard Peter call. He was by some trees not far from the water. "Here it is," he said. "I've found the boat!"

They stood round and looked down at the boat. "Just as we thought," said Simon. "A very small dinghy with an outboard engine."

"We don't really know whose boat it is," said John. "Is there a name-plate on it? Sometimes a dinghy has a name-plate which tells you the owner's name. Let's have a careful look."

Simon and John looked round the outside of the boat, but no name-plate and no owner's name could be found. Then John looked inside the little dinghy.

"Here we are," he said. "I can see an envelope under the seat and it has a name on it." He picked up the envelope and looked in it. There was no letter inside. He turned the envelope over and read out the name "Ron Dare."

"That's the name the policeman gave," said Peter. "Ron Dare is the name of the missing boy."

"I can't read any more because part of the envelope is wet," said John.

"It's enough," said Simon. "It's enough to tell us that this is the missing boat, and that Ron Dare is on the island."

They decided to make a search of the island for the boy. When they found him they would tell him that they wanted to help him. They agreed that it would be best to search the summer house first.

"Keep a careful look-out," said Simon to the others, as they started to walk up the hill towards the summer house.

"Yes," said John. "The boy doesn't know that we want to be friends with him. If he sees us he may be frightened and hide or run away. How can we let him know that we want to be friendly?"

"We could call out when we see him," said Jane. "We could call his name and say we are friends."

"That may not stop him running away if he's frightened," said Simon. "Perhaps we could leave a message in writing somewhere. We could leave one in his boat."

Then they decided to go back to the little dinghy and leave a message in it. They were afraid that the boy might get to the boat before they were able to talk to him.

John wrote a message on a piece of paper. It said "To Ron Dare. We are friends. We want to help you. Come to the summer house on the hill. Simon, John, Jane, Peter."

They pinned the paper to the seat of the dinghy and then they all started off up the hill again.

When they arrived at the summer house they made a quick search of all the rooms. However, there seemed to be no sign of Ron Dare.

One of the windows was open, but Jane remembered they had left it open the last time they were there.

They all went to talk things over in the room with the big window. Then they decided to make a more careful search of the house. "I don't think the boy is in the house now," said Simon, "but we ought to know if he's been here. Let's look in each room very carefully."

John went to look round the outside of the house. He soon appeared outside the window which had been left open. "There's a footprint out here below the window," he said. "It looks like the one we found on the beach. Perhaps Ron Dare got into the house by this open window."

They heard Jane calling from the kitchen and they went in to see her. "Some tins of food are missing," she told them.

"Are you sure?" Simon asked.

"Oh yes," Jane answered. "I remember that I counted fourteen tins when we were here last time, and now there are only nine."

Peter counted the tins in the cupboard. "Yes," he said. "There are only nine. Look, there's some money by the tins. Whose is it?"

"There was no money the last time we were here," said Jane. "The boy must have left it."

"Perhaps he wanted to pay for the tins he took," said John. "It may be his way of trying to be honest. It must be hard to be honest when you're on the run."

Simon said that they should start to search the island. First they went to look through the telescope in the big room. They took turns to look through it at the woods and the beach, but nothing could be seen of the boy.

"He's somewhere down there. Oh, I do wish we could find him," said Jane.

As Peter was having a last look through the telescope he suddenly said, "I can see a boat. I think it's a Police launch."

Soon they could all see the blue launch. At first they thought it was coming to the island, but then they could see that it was going fast towards the mainland.

"Perhaps it's been looking for Ron Dare," said Peter.

Before they started their search of the woods, they left another message for the missing boy. They pinned this on the door of the house as they went out. It read—"To Ron Dare. You can stay here. We've left the door open. We'll come back to see you and to help you. We're your friends.

Simon, John, Jane, Peter."

Simon and John led the way to the woods. They went straight to a look-out post they had made in a very tall tree. They had put a platform near the top of the tree. A rope ladder led to the platform.

John went up the rope ladder first. Then Peter went up more slowly after him. He was careful, so that there would be no accident. Simon went up the ladder last. Jane stayed on the ground to keep watch.

There was only room for three on the platform of the look-out post. As the tree was very tall they could see a long way from the platform.

For some minutes they looked around. Then suddenly they saw someone appear near the trees by the beach. It was a boy. He was walking towards their boat.

Simon stayed up the tree to watch, while John climbed quickly to the ground. He then ran straight towards the beach where they had left their dinghy.

Peter came slowly down the rope ladder. Then Jane and Peter both followed John to the beach, moving as quickly as they could.

Simon could see what was happening from the platform of the look-out post. He watched the boy go to their dinghy and look at it. Then he saw him looking out to sea towards their motor boat where it was tied to the buoy.

Suddenly the boy turned his head. He had heard John coming through the trees. He ran quickly along the beach and disappeared into the woods. When John came on to the beach there was nobody to be seen.

Simon called out to John, but he couldn't be heard as he was too far away. John waited for his two cousins. He knew they'd followed him. When they joined him, he told them that the boy had disappeared by the time he'd got to the beach. Then the three started back to join Simon and search the woods.

Peter, Jane and their two cousins started their search for Ron Dare at the place where he had disappeared into the woods. They spread out for the search, each one walking some distance from the others. They tried to cover the whole woods like this. However, some parts of the woods were very thick and it was hard to keep moving.

It took a long time to cover the whole of the woods in this way. As they were spread out they couldn't talk to each other and the two young children grew very tired of the search. They were glad when Simon called them together.

None of them had any news about the boy. They'd seen no sign of him.

Simon said, "Well, we've tried very hard to find the boy and we've covered all the woods in our search. It's going to get dark soon, so we must start to go home now."

They went back to the beach to their boat. Before they got into it, John wrote another message. He wrote it in the sand with a stick. It was, "We will come back soon. Your friends,

Simon, John, Peter, Jane."

On the way back in the motor boat they talked about the search they'd made. Simon said, "It's a mystery to me how we missed the boy when we searched the woods. We covered the whole woods, even the thick parts."

"Yes," said John, "it's a mystery to me, too. He must have been hiding in the woods as we went through them."

"Perhaps there's a hollow tree in the woods," said Simon. "If he'd found a hollow tree he could have been in it as we went by."

"Yes, even if we had gone very close we wouldn't have seen him," said Jane. She looked back at the island in the distance. "Poor boy," she said. "He must be lonely. I do wish we'd found him."

"He must see one of our messages," said Peter, "and we've left the house open for him. He has enough food to eat and somewhere to sleep. We'll find him tomorrow."

They decided to call in at the village Police Station to tell the policeman what had been happening on the island. They hoped the policeman would let them try to find the boy again the next day.

Simon led the way into the village Police Station. "We've news about the missing boy," he told the policeman there. "He's somewhere on the island."

"Oh," said the policeman. "He's appeared, has he? He took the little motor boat to get there, I suppose."

"Yes," said Simon, "but he's done nothing wrong. It was his own boat, you remember. He's an honest boy. He took some of our tins of food but left the money to pay for them."

"Did you talk to him?" asked the policeman.

"We tried to," said John, "but we couldn't get near him. We followed him into some woods but he disappeared. It's a mystery to us where he went."

"I suppose we'll have to get the Police launch out tomorrow, and go to find him," said the policeman.

Simon explained that this would need many men and take a long time. The policeman agreed. Then Simon said that he and his brother, with Peter and Jane, could find the boy in a day or two. He explained about the messages they had left for the boy. "We would keep in touch with you and tell you what is happening," he said.

The policeman got out some paper and wrote out a report on what he had been told about the missing boy.

"I'll have to get in touch with the boy's father," he said. "I'll telephone this report to him and see what he says. After all, the boy has done nothing very wrong, and it may be better if you find him. You wait here for a while."

Peter and Jane and their cousins sat down to wait while the policeman used the telephone. They heard him talk to Mr Dare and explain what had happened. Then Mr Dare spoke for some time.

At last the policeman put the telephone down and spoke to Simon and John. "Mr Dare is delighted to hear that his son has been found," he said. "He's very pleased with you and he wants you to get in touch with the boy tomorrow. He'll be able to come down himself in a day or two. He wants us to telephone him every day. He'll pay for the calls and anything else needed."

The children were delighted as they left the Police Station. "There's no need to worry now," said Jane.

The next day they made an early start for the island. Their motor boat left the mainland at nine o'clock.

Once on the island, they made straight for the place where the dinghy with the outboard engine was hidden. They wanted to see if the boy had taken the message they'd left pinned to the seat.

To their surprise the boat had gone. There were marks on the sand where it had been pulled down to the water.

John spoke first. "Oh dear!" he said. "He's gone. Do you suppose he's left the island?"

"We can't tell," answered Simon. "He may have hidden the boat in a different place."

"Why couldn't he wait for us?" asked Jane. "Why doesn't he want to be friendly?"

"He doesn't know us," said John. "I think he's frightened of us."

"Of course," said Jane. "Poor boy! He's lonely and frightened. We must find him quickly."

Simon told the others to search for the boat again. Before long they found it hidden under some bushes. The marks it had made in the sand had been smoothed away.

Then they went through the woods towards the summer house. On the way they found a hollow tree.

"It's still early," said Simon. "If the boy is still in the summer house we may surprise him. Let's get there quickly."

When they were near to the house they hid in the bushes some distance away and looked for signs of the missing boy. However, they couldn't see any smoke or anyone moving in the house, so they left the bushes and entered through the front door.

On their way in they noticed that their message had been taken from the front door.

They quickly looked round inside the house. Jane counted the tins of food. There were five instead of nine. Peter noticed that one of the beds had been used.

John called out, "My fishing rod is missing. Let's go down to the stream. We'll catch him there." They hurried from the house towards the stream. They thought that the boy might be catching some fish for breakfast. However, they were wrong.

Ron Dare was some distance away, climbing up the rope ladder to the look-out post in the tall tree. When he saw the motor boat by the buoy he hurriedly climbed down to the ground.

The game of hide and seek continued all the morning.

Peter and Jane had to be at their own home by dinner time, as they were going out with their uncle to the airfield for the afternoon. Simon and John also had to leave the island early, as they had work to do at home for their father.

As they left the island, they agreed to return the next day to continue the search. Simon said he would think of a plan to find Ron Dare. He said that perhaps they would need to stay on the island all day.

Peter and Jane were taken to the airfield by their uncle in a car. He'd promised some time ago to take them up in an aeroplane. On the way to the airfield Peter sat in the front of the car by his uncle, and Jane sat in the back. As they went along they told their uncle about the missing boy and their search of the island. Uncle and the two children continued talking as they parked their car and walked across the airfield.

Suddenly Peter and Jane noticed that their uncle was taking them towards a helicopter. They were surprised and delighted to know that they were going up in a helicopter.

The two children and their uncle got into the helicopter. Uncle showed them the safety straps on each seat. "We must fasten these safety straps," he said. "Please put them on now."

As they fastened the safety straps, Uncle explained how useful they were in times of accident.

They sat back and looked out of the helicopter as Uncle made it rise in the air.

"It seems to rise quickly," said Jane to Peter. "I didn't know that helicopters could go so fast."

"We can see a long way," Peter said. "Is that the island in the distance?" he asked. His uncle answered that it was, and said that he would fly the helicopter that way.

Soon they were flying over the island. "This is useful," said Peter, looking down. "We may be able to see the boy."

Uncle made the helicopter fly low so that it was near the tops of the trees. Suddenly they saw the boy. He was in the woods looking up at them. Then he disappeared.

"He must have jumped into that hollow tree again," said Peter. He explained to his uncle how the boy had hidden in a hollow tree during the search for him the day before.

By this time Uncle had become very interested in the boy on the island. "That poor boy must be lonely down there," he said. "Let's send him a message by parachute. I have a small parachute to use for that. I'll have to land so that I can write."

He made the helicopter land on the sands, took out a pencil and paper and wrote a long message for the boy. Peter and Jane sat still and answered Uncle's questions as he wrote. Then he put the message in a tin and fastened it to the small parachute.

Uncle started the engine and made the helicopter take off again. It kept low as it moved along.

They looked down and saw the boy again as he hurried up the hill. Uncle threw the parachute out of the helicopter as they went by. It opened at once and came down slowly in front of the running boy. They could see no more.

They landed on the airfield soon after and they thanked their uncle very much for taking them up in the helicopter.

As they got out Uncle said, "I kept the promise I made to you a long time ago."

The next day the cousins met Peter and Jane early. Before they left the mainland they sat in the motor boat and talked about Simon's plan to find Ron Dare.

First Simon spoke of his plan and then the others asked him questions about it.

He said that they must get to the island and reach the house before the boy knew they were there. They would hide quietly in the house until the boy entered. To do this they would have to go to the island a different way, and reach the house from the other side.

"It sounds like a good plan," said John. "Let's start now."

On the way to the island Peter and Jane told their cousins about their flight in a helicopter with their uncle. Peter said, "Uncle flew low over the island and we saw the boy twice."

"Yes," said Jane, "we saw him twice as we flew over, and each time he looked frightened. Uncle threw him a message with a parachute."

"That sounds very interesting," said Simon. "I hope the boy read the message."

When they reached the island, they made their way quietly to the house and entered by the back way. They didn't see the boy.

Simon, John and their two cousins waited quietly in the house for Ron Dare to appear. When they spoke they did so very quietly as they didn't want to frighten away their expected visitor. They wanted him to come into the room before he knew they were there.

"I've given the Police a report each day, as I promised," said Simon. "The policeman again told me to keep in touch with him. He expects Mr Dare to arrive later today."

"I expect he'll want to take his son back with him," said John. "I do hope we can bring father and son together."

Suddenly Simon made a sign for them all to keep quiet. He had heard a noise outside. Then the others heard a noise. Someone had opened the front door of the house. Their visitor had arrived. Simon moved across the room without a sound. He reached the door and stood to one side of it.

The door opened and Ron Dare walked in. He stood still when he saw the others.

"Hallo," said John. Then Peter and Jane said, "Hallo."

"Hallo," said the boy. He turned to go, but Simon had moved between him and the door.

Jane noticed that Ron wore dirty clothes and that he looked tired. "We've come to help you," she said quietly. "We want to be your friends. There's nothing to fear."

The boy wanted to ask questions. "Who are you?" he asked. "Whose house is this? Are you the owners? What do you know about me?"

"Suppose you sit down here between Peter and me, and tell us all about it," said Jane.

The boy appeared to like Jane and the others and he seemed to have lost his fear. He started to tell them his story and he talked for a long time. He stood up at first but later sat down.

His story was that his mother had died several years ago. He had lived happily with his father until recently. Then his father went away for a long time on business. Ron had to live with an uncle he didn't like. He felt he couldn't live happily with him so he ran away. His father had a holiday house near the island and he had gone to that at first. Then a policeman had called there and had nearly caught him.

"I'm glad I've been caught now," he said.

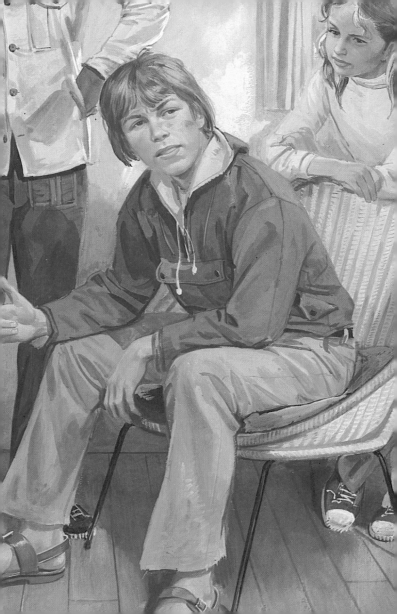

Several minutes later they were on their way back to the mainland. There they called at the Police Station to report what had happened. The policeman told them that Mr Dare had not arrived.

"We're all going to our house now," said Simon.

"All right," replied the policeman. "I'll tell Mr Dare where you are, when he comes."

"Will your father be angry with you?" Jane asked Ron on their way to the house.

"No, it'll be all right. He won't be angry," replied Ron. "I'm sorry that I've made him worry."

It wasn't long before Mr Dare arrived. He was very happy to see his son again. Ron told him at once how sorry he was for giving him so much worry.

Mr Dare said that Ron was coming back to live with him as he wasn't going away on business again for some time. He also said that a kind aunt whom Ron liked was coming to live with them.

Mr Dare thanked Simon, John, Jane and Peter for helping to find his son again. He had been worried recently but there was a happy ending to the story.

New words used in this book

Total number of new words 129

Peter and Jane had a letter from Ron after he'd gone back to his own home to live with his father. It was a long letter and they were glad to find it was a happy one. From his letter it seemed that all his worries had disappeared.

He wrote about the days when he was hiding on the island. Jane read out part of the letter to Peter —

"I was most frightened the day the helicopter came. It came down so low over me I was afraid it might land on top of me. The noise made me even more frightened. For a while I thought that the Police were in the helicopter. I didn't know what the little parachute was at first. I'd never seen anyone send a message like that before. It was kind of your uncle to write the message. Perhaps he'll let me have a ride in his helicopter one day. I hope to see you all when I come on holiday."

"We should send this letter to Uncle," said Peter. "He was very interested in the missing boy on the island. He'll be pleased to know it all ended happily."